THE ADVENTURES OF Captain Pugwash

Hot Chocolate

RED
FOX

A Red Fox Book

Published by Random House Children's Books
20 Vauxhall Bridge Road, London SW1V 2SA

A division of The Random House Group Ltd
London Melbourne Sydney Auckland
Johannesburg and agencies throughout the world

The Adventures of Captain Pugwash
Created by John Ryan
© Britt Allcroft (Development) Limited 2000
All rights worldwide Britt Allcroft (Development) Limited
CAPTAIN PUGWASH is a trademark of Britt Allcroft (Development) Limited
THE BRITT ALLCROFT COMPANY is a trademark of The Britt Allcroft Company plc

Cover illustration by Ian Hillyard
Inside illustrations by Red Central Limited

Text adapted by Sally Byford from the original TV story

1 3 5 7 9 10 8 6 4 2

Printed in Hong Kong by Midas Printing Ltd

THE RANDOM HOUSE GROUP Limited Reg. No. 954009

www.randomhouse.co.uk

ISBN 0 09 941303 5

Captain Pugwash's piggy bank was nearly empty and he was feeling very gloomy. He decided to buy a large bar of chocolate to cheer himself up.

The Governor of Portobello was also short of money, so he decided to increase the price of every chocolate bar in town by five doubloons. He put Lieutenant Scratchwood in charge of collecting the money, and anyone caught bringing in chocolate from other islands would be thrown into jail.

Scratchwood marched into town, where he met Pugwash gobbling his chocolate bar.

"Halt!" shouted Scratchwood. Then he ordered Pugwash to pay the extra five doubloons for his chocolate.

"Certainly not," said Pugwash crossly.

"Pay up or I'll throw you in jail," said Scratchwood.

"Stuttering starfish," grumbled Pugwash, handing over a bag of coins. "That's my last five doubloons."

Pugwash walked back to the Black Pig. He didn't see Cut-throat Jake and Rook, the thief, whispering together by the harbour. Rook was trying to persuade Jake to bring in some chocolate from another island.

"I'm not doing that. I'd be a fool. Scratchwood is searching all the boats in the bay," said Jake. "But I know someone who might. Captain Pugwash!"

So Rook went to the Black Pig and asked Captain Pugwash
if he'd do the job.

"You want me to sail to Faticoco, collect the chocolate and
then deliver it to you at Bounty Bay," whispered Pugwash.
"I can't possibly do that."

Rook held out a purse full of money. "There'll be more
when you get back," he said.

"Shivering sharks," said Pugwash. "I'll do it. We'll set sail
this evening."

Meanwhile, Cut-throat Jake had thought of a wicked plan
to trick his old enemy, Pugwash.

"We'll wait until he is sailing to Bounty Bay with his ship
full of chocolate, and then we'll attack!" Jake told his crew.

Dook, Swine and Stinka cheered.

"Then we'll steal the chocolate and sell it ourselves,"
chuckled Jake. "That way Pugwash does all the hard work
and we make all the money!"

That night, the Black Pig reached
the little island of Faticoco. Pugwash
collected the chocolate and Jonah and
Willy heaved it on board with a pulley.
    The crate was high up in the air,
when Pugwash came on deck carrying
a small block of chocolate. "Never
mind that, Jonah," he said. "Give me
a hand."

As Jonah rushed to help the Captain, he let go of the rope. The crate was too heavy for Willy to hold on his own, and he flew into the air. The crate crashed onto the deck, spilling chocolate everywhere, and Willy landed in the middle of it. He picked up a bar and took a bite.

"Tottering turtles!" cried Pugwash. "Don't eat it! Clear it up and stow it in the hold."

At last the chocolate was safely stored in the hold, and the Black Pig was sailing back to Bounty Bay. The night was getting hotter and hotter and none of the crew could sleep. They couldn't stop thinking about all that chocolate.

"The Captain said we mustn't eat any," said the Mate.

"But he's eaten loads," said Willy.

"He won't notice if we take a little bit," said Jonah. "Let's go now while he's asleep."

Jonah, Willy and the Mate crept quietly into the hold. In the dark, they didn't see Pugwash, who was already there, eating the chocolate. Suddenly they bumped into him.

"Help!" they screamed, while Pugwash ran and hid behind the chocolate.

Tom rushed in with a lantern and Pugwash popped up from his hiding place. He was very annoyed to see his crew. "I'd better guard this chocolate myself from now on," he said. "Move it to the galley, Tom."

"It's very hot in there, Captain," said Tom, but Pugwash took no notice.

The next day was even hotter. Below deck, the Mate had noticed a brown drip falling from the ceiling. "Get that cleared up, will you, Tom," he said.

Tom fetched a bucket to catch the drips. When no one was looking, he caught some on his finger and tasted it.

"Just as I thought!" said Tom. "It's so hot in the galley that the chocolate is melting."

While Pugwash guarded the galley, Tom secretly collected all the melted chocolate in buckets.

At last they reached Bounty Bay, where Rook was waiting to collect the cargo.

"It's all here safe and sound," Pugwash told Rook. "But it's awfully hot. How about a drink before we unload?"

Rook agreed and followed Pugwash to his cabin.

Meanwhile, Willy had spotted Scratchwood and his soldiers rowing towards them.

"It looks like we've got visitors," said Willy.

Tom looked in the other direction, and saw Cut-throat Jake and his crew rowing towards them, too.

"It's worse than I thought," whispered Tom. "Not just the soldiers, but Jake as well."

Scratchwood and his soldiers climbed aboard the ship as Pugwash and Rook came back on deck.

"The Governor has ordered me to search this ship for chocolate," announced Scratchwood.

Pugwash was horrified. "B-b-but you can't do that," he stuttered, while Rook quickly slipped away.

Scratchwood ignored Pugwash, and the soldiers started
their search. When they saw that the galley was locked,
they smashed down the door. Pugwash trembled with fear
as the soldiers followed him in.

But, to Pugwash's amazement, the galley was empty.
The chocolate had gone!

"Stuttering starfish!" he cried, as the soldiers marched
off to search the rest of the ship.

By now Jake and his crew had reached the Black Pig in their long boat.

"Let's attack!" roared Jake.

Tom was waiting with the buckets of melted chocolate. Quickly, he emptied them over Dook, Swine and Stinka until they were covered in a thick layer of chocolate. Jake roared with laughter – until Tom threw a bucket over him, too.

"Wait till I get you," growled Jake.

At that moment, Scratchwood marched up, with Pugwash scurrying along behind him.

"I can smell chocolate," said Scratchwood.

"N-n-no, it must be the seaweed," stuttered Pugwash.

Tom pointed to Jake and his crew. "You'll find lots of chocolate in that long boat," he said.

Scratchwood looked down at Jake's boat. "It's the chocolate thieves!" he cried. "Soldiers, arrest those men and throw them in jail!" He turned to Tom. "Well done, young fellow."

"Yes, Tom, not bad, for a cabin boy," said Pugwash, with surprise.

While Cut-throat Jake was stuck in jail, Pugwash and his crew celebrated with chocolate cake, chocolate biscuits and mugs of hot chocolate.

Tom told Pugwash that the chocolate had melted in the galley.

"And whose idea was it to store the chocolate there?" asked Pugwash proudly.

"Yours of course," said Tom, and all the crew cheered.